THE GRUFFALO

For all at Auchterhouse Primary School—J.D.

PUFFIN BOOKS
An imprint of Penguin Random House LLC
375 Hudson Street
New York, New York 10014

Originally published in Great Britain by Macmillan Children's Books, 1999
First published in the United States of America by Dial Books for Young Readers,
a division of Penguin Putnam Inc., 1999
Published by Puffin Books, a division of Penguin Young Readers Group, 2006

Text copyright © 1999 by Julia Donaldson
Pictures copyright © 1999 by Axel Scheffler

LIBRARY OF CONGRESS CATALOGING IN PUBLICATION DATA IS AVAILABLE UPON REQUEST.

Puffin Books ISBN 9780142403877

Manufactured in China
The art was created using pencil, ink, watercolors, colored pencils, and crayons.

38

THE GRUFFALO

Julia Donaldson
pictures by Axel Scheffler

PUFFIN BOOKS

A mouse took a stroll through the deep dark wood.

A fox saw the mouse and the mouse looked good.

"Where are you going to, little brown mouse?

Come and have lunch in my underground house."

"It's terribly kind of you, Fox, but no—

I'm going to have lunch with a gruffalo."

"A gruffalo? What's a gruffalo?"

"A gruffalo! Why, didn't you know?"

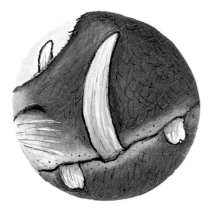

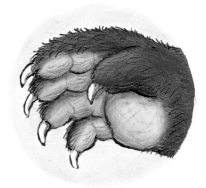

"He has terrible tusks,   and terrible claws,

and terrible teeth in his terrible jaws."

"*Where are you meeting him?*"
"Here, by these rocks . . .
and his favorite food is roasted fox."

"Roasted fox! Oh, my!" Fox said.
"Good-bye, little mouse," and away he sped.

"Silly old Fox! Doesn't he know?
There's no such thing as a gruffalo!"

On went the mouse through the deep dark wood.

An owl saw the mouse and the mouse looked good.

"Where are you going to, little brown mouse?

Join me for tea in my treetop house."

"It's frightfully nice of you, Owl, but no—

I'm going to have tea with a gruffalo."

"A gruffalo? What's a gruffalo?"

"A gruffalo! Why, didn't you know?"

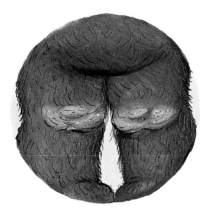

"He has knobbly knees,

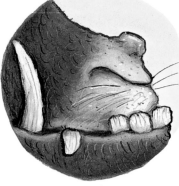

and turned-out toes,

and a poisonous wart at the end of his nose."

"*Where are you meeting him?*"
"Here, by this stream . . .
    and his favorite food is owl ice cream."

"Owl ice cream? Too-whit! Too-whoo!
Good-bye, little mouse," and away Owl flew.

"Silly old Owl! Doesn't he know?
There's no such thing as a gruffalo!"

On went the mouse through the deep dark wood.

A snake saw the mouse and the mouse looked good.

"Where are you going to, little brown mouse?

Come for a feast in my log-pile house."

"It's wonderfully good of you, Snake, but no—

I'm having a feast with a gruffalo."

"A gruffalo? What's a gruffalo?"

"A gruffalo! Why, didn't you know?"

"His eyes are orange.

His tongue is black.

He has purple prickles all over his back."

"Where are you meeting him?"
"Here, by this lake . . .
and his favorite food is scrambled snake."

"Scrambled snake? It's time I hid!
Good-bye, little mouse," and away Snake slid.

"Silly old Snake! Doesn't he know?
There's no such thing as a gruffal . . .

"Oh!"

But who is this creature with terrible claws,
and terrible teeth in his terrible jaws?
He has knobbly knees and turned-out toes,
and a poisonous wart at the end of his nose.
His eyes are orange, his tongue is black;
he has purple prickles all over his back.

"Oh, help! Oh, no!
IT'S A GRUFFALO!"

"*My favorite food!*" the gruffalo said.
"*You'll taste good on a slice of bread!*"

"Good?" said the mouse. "Don't call me good!
I'm the scariest creature in this deep dark wood.
Just walk behind me and soon you'll see,
everyone is afraid of me."

"*Oh, sure!*" said the gruffalo, bursting with laughter.
"*You lead the way and I'll follow after.*"

They walked and walked till the gruffalo said,
"*I hear a hiss in the grass ahead.*"

"It's Snake," said the mouse. "Why, Snake, hello!"
Snake took one look at the gruffalo.
"*Oh, dear!*" he said, "*good-bye, little mouse,*"
and slid right into his log-pile house.

"You see?" said Mouse. "I told you so."
"Amazing!" said the gruffalo.

They walked some more till the gruffalo said,
"I hear a hoot in the trees ahead."

"It's Owl," said the mouse. "Why, Owl, hello!"
Owl took one look at the gruffalo.
"Boo-whoo!" he said, *"good-bye, little mouse,"*
and flew right up to his treetop house.

"You see?" said Mouse. "I told you so."
"*Astounding!*" said the gruffalo.

They walked some more till the gruffalo said,
"*I hear some paws on the path ahead.*"

"It's Fox," said the mouse. "Why, Fox, hello!"
Fox took one look at the gruffalo.
"Oh, help!" he said, *"good-bye, little mouse,"*
and ran right into his underground house.

The mouse said, "Gruffalo, now you see,
everyone is afraid of me!
But now my tummy is starting to rumble,
and my favorite food is . . . gruffalo crumble!"

"*Gruffalo crumble!*" the gruffalo said,
and quick as the wind he turned and fled.

All was quiet in the deep dark wood.

The mouse found a nut and the nut was good.